A Good Day, A Good Night

For my aunt, Patty Dingus,
for Mr. Bost—and for Patrick.

A Good Day,
A Good Night

by Cindy Wheeler

J.B. Lippincott   New York

LIBRARY OF CONGRESS CATALOGING IN PUBLICATION DATA
Wheeler, Cindy. A good day, a good night.
SUMMARY: A robin and a cat have a good day followed by a good night.
[1. Robins—Fiction. 2. Cats—Fiction]
I. Title.
PZ7.W5593Go 1980   [E]   79-3017
ISBN 0-397-31900-2   ISBN 0-397-31901-0 lib. bdg.

FIRST EDITION

A GOOD DAY

The sun is up.

Robin is up.

Marmalade is up.

Marmalade sees Robin.

Robin flies away.

Robin has food.

Marmalade wants food.

Marmalade gets milk.

Marmalade is happy.

Robin is happy.

This is a good day.

A GOOD NIGHT

The sun is going to bed.

Robin is going to bed.

Lightning Bug is getting up.

Bat is getting up.

Rabbit is getting up.

Marmalade wants to play.

Time for bed, Marmalade!

"Good night."

This is a good night.

Cindy Wheeler grew up in Alabama, Virginia, and North Carolina. She spent her early years on Buzzard Rock, a mountaintop in North Carolina, along with her family, bears, wildcats, a dog, and a cat (who slept in the bird feeder). Ms. Wheeler has a B.F.A. degree from Auburn University. She is currently living and working in New York City. *A Good Day, A Good Night* is her first book.